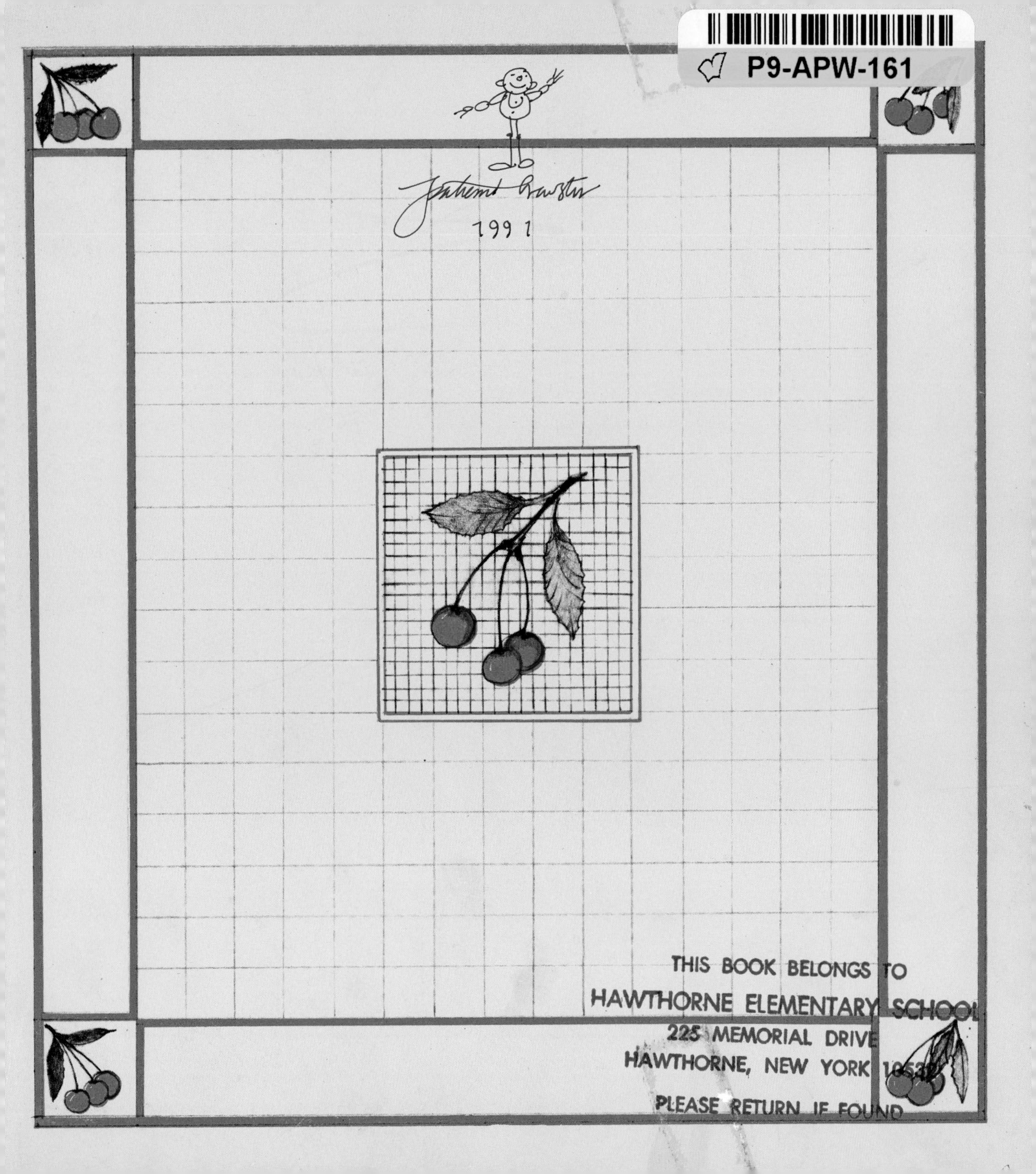

NOBODY

BY PATIENCE BREWSTER

CLARION BOOKS
TICKNOR & FIELDS: A HOUGHTON MIFFLIN COMPANY
New York

Nobody is dedicated to
his creator (and mine), my mother;
and to his friend (and mine),
my sister Sarah.

Clarion Books
Ticknor & Fields, a Houghton Mifflin Company

Printed in U.S.A.

Library of Congress Cataloging in Publication Data

Brewster, Patience. Nobody.
Summary: Although Sarah frequently claims "Nobody did it," no one is more surprised than she when Nobody is finally revealed to be somebody.
[1. Behavior—Fiction] I. Title.
PZ7.B7572N. [E] 82-1302
ISBN 0-89919-110-X AACR2
Y 10 9 8 7 6 5 4 3 2

Once there was a little girl named Sarah, who sometimes had terrible, good-for-nothing days. She had one of those days just a week before her birthday.

Nothing had gone right, and by
the time she came home from school,
Sarah was very grumpy.

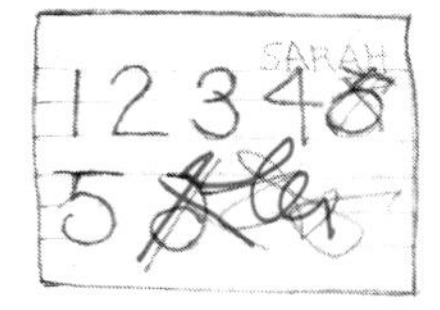

Mommy took one look at her and said, "Sarah, who are you frowning at?"

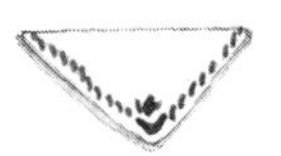

"Nobody," mumbled Sarah.

"Well," said Mommy, "tell me about school today. Who passed out the crackers at snack time?"

"Nobody," grumbled Sarah.

Mommy thought for a minute.

Then she said, "If Nobody passed out the crackers, then Nobody spilled the crackers, so Nobody had to pick them up. That Nobody must have been very busy today."

Sarah scowled. Then she began to smile as she imagined a funny Nobody doing all those things.

“What does Nobody look like?” asked Mommy. “Can you draw me a picture?” Sarah got out her best pencil and a big piece of paper.

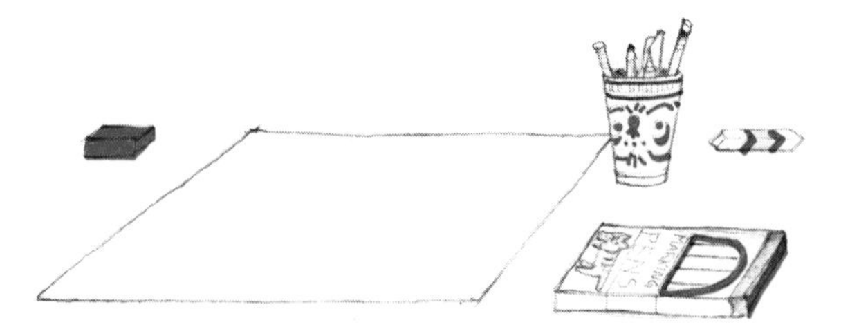

This is the picture she drew.

After that, Nobody was with Sarah all the time.

On Saturday, who do you suppose
came to play with Sarah?

Nobody.

Sarah told Nobody stories and sang songs to Nobody.
She had a tea party and Nobody was invited.

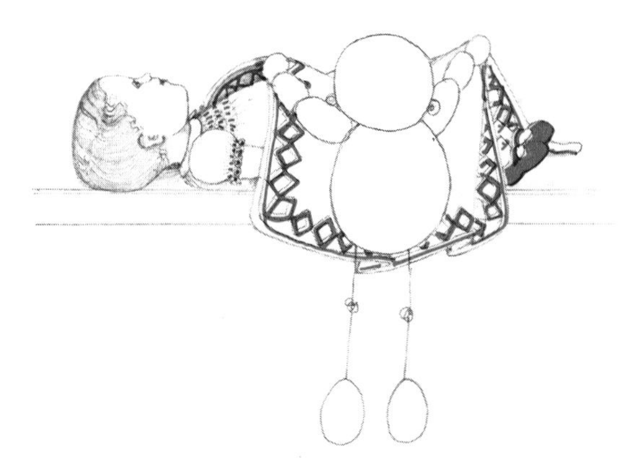

On Sunday, Sarah looked all over the house for her doll Ellis.

Nobody had hidden her, so Sarah found Ellis right where she had left her.

On Monday, who waited for
the school bus with Sarah?

Nobody.

While Sarah waited, she had Nobody to talk to.

On Tuesday, Miss Fosdick said, "Nobody is sick today." All the children cheered except Sarah.

She felt sorry for Nobody. How would you feel if everyone was glad you were sick?

On Wednesday, Sarah bumped her elbow. It hurt and she started to cry. Daddy said, "Listen. Who's crying?"

Sarah listened quietly. Who do you suppose was crying then?

Nobody, of course.

On Thursday, Sarah was in a hurry.
She left her room in a mess.

Guess who helped her clean up when
she came home from school?

Nobody.

On Friday, when Sarah was tucked in bed for the night, she heard funny noises. She thought she saw the curtain move. But Sarah wasn't frightened.

She knew Nobody was there.

Saturday was Sarah's birthday. She had friends over for cake and ice cream. They brought her some very nice presents. It was a wonderful party.

After everyone had gone home, Sarah looked at all her new things and noticed a gift that Nobody had wrapped. She opened it up, and guess what...?

Nobody was inside!

Sarah was very happy. Now Nobody really was somebody.